The Edge Is Burning

by

Paul Kropp

LIBRARY AND ARCHIVES CANADA CATALOGUING IN PUBLICATION

Kropp, Paul, 1948–

    The edge is burning / Paul Kropp.

(HIP edge)
ISBN 978-1-897039-33-5

    I. Title. II. Series.

PS8571.R772E34 2008   jC813'.54   C2008-902050-2

General editor: Paul Kropp
Text design: Laura Brady
Illustrations drawn by: Catherine Doherty
Cover design: Robert Corrigan

1 2 3 4 5 6 7   13 12 11 10 09 08

Printed and bound in Canada

High Interest Publishing acknowledges the financial support of the Government of Canada through the Book Publishing Industry Development Program (BPIDP) for our publishing activities.

Someone is burning down houses in Edgemont. First Nick loses his house. Then a fire starts next to his friend's place. Nick knows it's arson, but the cops don't believe him.

CHAPTER ONE

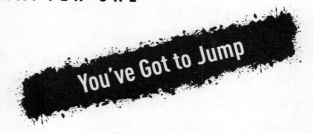

You've Got to Jump

I was lying in my bed, mostly asleep. The earphones had popped out of my ears. My eyes were pretty much closed. My brain had gone off somewhere. A dream. I was dreaming about being trapped in a dark room, trying to get out. I kept fighting to get out, but I was trapped . . . and then I woke up. The sheets were all twisted around me. I was sweating. But I was back in real life.

In real life, I smelled something. Something like smoke.

My eyes popped open and I sniffed again. Yes, it was smoke. Something in the house was burning. It could be my mom making something in the kitchen. Nah, she was at work. Or maybe it was my little brother, Jackson. Maybe the kid was playing with matches again. Or maybe it was the old guy downstairs, on the first floor.

I sat up. Then I turned on the light by my bed. The air was a little foggy in the room, or maybe my eyes were foggy. No way to tell. I rubbed my eyes, then looked around and tried to sniff some more.

No, it wasn't just burned food. It smelled . . . different.

Then the smoke alarm went off. That was no surprise. The smoke alarm would go off if you cooked bacon too long in the morning. So now I had the smell of smoke and the alarm going beep-beep-beep-beep.

Forget sleeping. I rubbed my eyes, then saw smoke coming in under the door to the hall.

Holy ——, I said to myself. *This is real.*

"Jackson, can you hear me?" I shouted to my little brother. Jackson is eight; I'm sixteen. I'm supposed to be smarter.

There was no answer. I tried again, "Jackson, can you hear me? Say something!"

Nothing. Just beep-beep-beep-beep.

I got out of bed and tried to think. Okay, so there's a fire. There's smoke coming in under the door. What are you supposed to do if smoke comes in like that? *Think,* I told myself.

Get out of the house. Yeah, that's number one. *Cover your mouth, then get out of the house.* But what about my brother? He's only eight and he'll probably hide under his bed. I've got to go get him. But there's smoke out in the hall, and it's the smoke that kills you. That's what the TV ads always say, it's the smoke that kills you.

Okay, so I needed a plan. The smoke alarm noise was going through my brain like a chainsaw. I had to think.

I saw a pair of underwear lying on the floor.

Actually, there were a lot of clothes on the floor, and my mom bugged me about that. But then I saw this T-shirt, and I saw a Coke can. Then I put two and two together. Get the T-shirt wet with the Coke. Put the T-shirt over my mouth. Then get over to Jackson's room and get him out.

Fast.

The Coke spritzed when I pulled the tab. Then it made a mess all over the T-shirt, but so what? I got up and was almost ready to leave when I stopped. Should I grab my coat? No. I put my hand on the doorknob and stopped again. *Check to see if the doorknob is hot.* I remembered that from someplace.

The doorknob was cold.

Show time, I said to myself. Then I turned the knob and rushed into the hall.

The whole house was filled with white smoke. The smoke stung my eyes and made me cough, despite my Coke-soaked T-shirt.

I had to feel my way down the hall. "Jackson!" I shouted, but there was no answer. At last I reached the door to his room. I turned the handle and pushed, but the door was locked. "Jackson, you in there?"

No answer. Just the beep of the fire alarm.

My brother always locked the door when he went to bed. It was a little two-buck lock, good for nothing, but still Jackson used it. Maybe he thought I'd come and beat him up in the middle of the night. Who knows what an eight-year-old thinks?

But I knew what was going on in my head. A couple million thoughts went through my brain all at once. I could picture Jackson downstairs, with matches, burning alive. I could picture him outside, laughing at all this. And I could picture him under his bed, scared to death.

"Jackson," I yelled again. But this time the intake of smoke made me cough.

I backed away from the door, then ran into it shoulder first.

The lock broke and I stepped inside. There was

less smoke here, so it was easier to see. "Jackson, you in here?" I yelled.

"Down here," I heard. The voice was muffled.

No surprise, the kid was under his bed.

I shut the door behind me to keep the smoke out. That was one smart thing. It would buy a little time.

"Come on," I said. "We've got to get out of here."

"There's smoke, Nick. There's fire."

"Yeah, I kind of figured that out," I snapped back. "We're going out the window. It's the only way."

"But . . ."

"No buts," I told him. "You're better off with a broken leg than getting burned alive. Now let's go."

So there we were, one teenager and one little kid in pajamas, both of us looking out a second-floor window. It wasn't that far down. I mean, I've done diving boards higher than our bedroom window. But it sure looks a long way down when you're scared. Jackson was scared.

"I can't do it."

"Yes, you can," I told him. "Just sit on the window, then push off. Bend your legs and roll when you hit the ground. There's nothing to it."

The kid just looked at me.

"C'mon," I begged. "You jump, then get out of the way. I'll be right after you."

I looked back at the door and saw smoke coming in. The smoke was darker now, almost black. I didn't like the look of that.

"I'm scared, Nick," Jackson whined. "How about you let me down on a rope?"

"Because we haven't got a rope, idiot! Now let's move."

"Okay, then use the bedsheet. I saw them do that once."

"Where?"

"On cartoons."

So I swore. I know I shouldn't swear in front of my little brother, but I did. The kid was just so stupid. There was smoke coming under the door

and he wanted to dangle off a sheet. But there was no time to argue. If the kid felt better hanging on to a sheet, let him have the sheet.

"Okay," I said, grabbing the sheet from his bed. "Let's go."

I twisted the sheet as best I could, then opened the window. I picked Jackson up and sat him on the window ledge, then gave him one end of the sheet. In the distance, I could hear sirens.

Was this smart? I wondered. Should I just wait for the firefighters?

No, it wasn't that far. When I ran out of sheet, Jackson would only fall maybe ten feet. That wouldn't even leave a bruise.

"Hold tight," I told him. "Now get your butt off the window sill."

"You won't let go?" he asked. He was really scared.

"I won't let go. Trust me."

So Jackson wiggled off the window sill. I could feel his weight on the sheet. The kid doesn't weigh much, but I had to fight to hold on. Then, slowly, I loosened my grip. The sheet zipped between my hands, ripping at my skin. At last, there was no more sheet.

I looked down. There was a yellow, flickering light coming from the house. The first floor was in flames. Soon it would burn up the stairs. I was running out of time.

"Okay, now you've got to jump the rest of the way. Get ready," I yelled.

"It's too far!" he cried.

"On the count of three, I'm letting go. One . . . two . . . three!"

I let go of the sheet, and heard my brother hit the soft ground below. I could hear him grunt and start crying. The sirens of the fire engines were very close. I could see the flashing light from the trucks.

I had to make up my mind – jump or wait. The firefighters might get me out in a minute or two. If I had a minute or two. But the first floor was already in flames. The smoke coming in under the door was black. If I jumped, I might break a leg. If I stayed put, I might end up dead.

"Get out of the way! I'm coming down!" I yelled.

Jackson was still crying, but I saw him move away. There were people from next door and down the street. One of them had a blanket to put around my brother.

"Watch out," I yelled as I got on the window sill. Then I counted: *one, two, three.* And I jumped.

That's the last part I remember.

CHAPTER TWO

It Wasn't an Accident

I didn't get to school the next day. They kept me at the hospital for "observation." I guess that means the nurses kept looking at me to make sure I wasn't really messed up.

And I wasn't really messed up. I didn't break my leg on the jump. But I did smash my head against the deck. Good thing I have a hard head and the deck is made of wood. So the good news was that Jackson and I were okay. My mom was all upset when they called her at work, but she was okay. And old Mr. Rouse downstairs got out in plenty of time.

But the bad news was this — we didn't have a house anymore. Not only that, we didn't have *anything*! Clothes, comics, games, baby pictures — all gone. Even the gerbil died, but I had never liked the gerbil much. He was Jackson's pet.

There were clips on the TV news that I saw in the hospital. It's pretty strange to sit in a bed and watch your own house burn, but there it was. The headlines were good, too: "Teenager and Kid Brother Jump for Their Lives." Too bad nobody caught that on video.

Not long after we jumped, the whole house went up in flames. It was really something. Kind of cool, if you're just watching the news . . . but not if it's your own house.

After we left the hospital, the Red Cross put all of us in a hotel room. The place was nice enough, but it was way outside the Edge. They gave us some clothes, too. Nothing cool, but enough to get by.

When I got to school on Tuesday, I looked pretty

ragged. I think all the kids at Edgemont had heard about the fire. They kept staring at me like I should have burn marks on my face.

I didn't get to see my buddy Marco until lunch. Good news – the Red Cross gave me money to buy lunch. Bad news – lunch was soggy fish and chips.

"Nice outfit," Marco said. That's the kind of guy he was – always with a smart-ass comment. Sometimes I wonder why he's my best friend.

"Red Cross hand-me-downs," I snapped back. I sat down beside him, then looked hard at the soggy fish on my tray.

"How's your little brother?"

"Upset about the gerbil."

Marco sighed. "I never liked that gerbil."

"Me neither."

"That fish looks kind of like fried gerbil."

That's when I stopped and stared at him. I mean, this was my lunch! And I'd just been through a pretty rough time. All the other kids looked at me like I was a victim. But my best friend makes me want to throw up my lunch.

Marco blinked and grinned. "Okay, sorry. But I've got an idea for you. Why not come live at my place until your mom gets stuff settled?"

"Your place?"

"Yeah, I asked my parents, and they're cool with it. We've got one of those blow-up beds. Unless you stick a pin in the thing, you'll be fine."

It was almost like Marco read my mind. The bus ride from the hotel to school was an hour, a lousy hour. I had to get up at six to get to school by eight thirty. And Marco's house was only half a block from mine . . . I mean, the house I used to have. I'd done sleepovers there lots of times. Besides, Marco had a Wii, and right now I had nothing. Nothing at all.

"Okay, thanks," I said.

"So tell me about it," he replied. He bit into a sandwich that his mom had made.

And I did. I told him about the fire, and getting out, and getting knocked out. Then I told him about the hospital and going to the hotel. I even told him I felt pretty bummed out, but I didn't make a big deal out of it. I mean, we're guys. We're supposed to be tough.

"You know," Marco said when I took a bite of my fish, "it wasn't an accident."

"Huh?"

"The fire at your place – it wasn't an accident."

"So what was it?"

"Arson," he said. "Somebody started the fire on purpose. It's all part of a pattern. Six fires on two streets in the Edge. All this year. I saw the map on TV. Six fires on two streets – that's no accident."

"You watch too much TV," I told him.

"That's what my mom says," Marco replied. "But she's wrong too."

After school, we walked back to my old house. The walls were made of brick, so they were still standing, but there was nothing left inside. The windows were

gone, the roof had fallen in, the house was toast. The fire was so hot that the people next door had to battle the flames. Their house looked scorched.

The place stunk. There's a smell to a burned out house that's pretty awful. A little fire, like a kitchen fire, that's nothing. The firefighters put it out, they set up a big fan to get out the smoke, and then – bang – you're back in.

But not my house. There was nothing to do but tear the place down.

Marco started to poke around. That was a good thing, because I was starting to lose it. Before this, I hadn't thought much about losing the house. I was too busy thinking about what would happen next. But now I looked at the old place – the place where I grew up – and I kind of lost it. Everything was gone. The marks on the kitchen wall to show how I grew. The collection of comics I was saving, because they'd be worth a lot some day. The funny rear porch where we used to throw toy army guys down to the yard. All of it – gone.

I started crying, not so anybody could see. Then I put a Kleenex right up to my face, to cover up. I pretended the smell was getting to me.

"Look over here," Marco called to me. "Look at this basement window."

"Yeah?"

"You say the fire started downstairs, right? And old Mr. Rouse doesn't smoke. He told the TV guys that the fire just came from nowhere. But I think it came from the basement."

"What are you? A CSI guy?"

Marco glared at me. "See how all the other windows blew their glass out. That's how it is with a fire. Big heat inside, the glass blows outside. But not here."

"Yeah?"

"So I think that somebody smashed the window, then started the fire in the basement. Right here."

I shook my head. "You should be a fire marshal." But Marco didn't even smile. "You think some crazy guy is going around, burning up the Edge?"

Marco just stared at me. "Who said he's crazy?" he asked me. "And how do you know he's a guy?"

Those were two pretty good questions. I didn't have answers. And I didn't know if Marco was right, or crazy himself.

CHAPTER THREE

Voices in the Night

I kind of liked living at Marco's house. It was a lot like my old house, but his family had the whole place. They even had a basement room where we could play Wii. So after school we'd finish our dumb homework and then play Wii boxing. Or sometimes it was the other way around . . . until his mom caught us.

My mom had gone off to live with her sister, and my little brother stayed with the two of them. But it would be tough for me to switch schools, so I stayed with Marco. That way I could keep going to Edgemont. Besides, Marco's parents were a lot nicer to me than my mom was. Maybe they felt sorry for me. I mean, I was a kid burned out of his own house. Or maybe they were just nice, just because they were.

Besides, I wouldn't be there long. Some city case worker was trying to find a place for us. Someplace in the Edge, so we wouldn't have to change schools. The case worker would have something in a couple of weeks, she said.

So Marco's place was my place, at least for a while. It was cool. We had always been friends. Now we were like brothers, except I got the cruddy bed.

I didn't sleep all that well. A blow-up bed is kind of bouncy. And it's kind of cold. And it gets saggy when the air comes out. So I would often toss and turn in the bed, long after Marco was snoring.

It was a week after the fire when I woke up around midnight. I had heard something. I wasn't sure what, but something. The dog next door barked a couple of times, and then I heard some footsteps out back. Why would somebody be out back that late?

So I got up and lifted the blind. Of course, I couldn't see a thing. But now I heard a voice – some whispers. I couldn't make out the words. In fact, the words didn't sound like English.

"What are you doing?" Marco asked. I guess I'd woken him up.

"Shhh!" I whispered. "Somebody's out back."

"Yeah, old Mrs. McNally's dogs."

"No, people," I whispered. "I heard them."

"You are so full of it," Marco grumbled. But he climbed out of his bed and came over beside me. Now we both stared out in the darkness.

Then we both heard something. It was two guys talking, but very quietly.

Very softly, Marco pushed the window open.

The two guys were still whispering, but now we could hear better. Not that their words made much sense. Whatever they spoke, it wasn't English.

"I'm calling the cops," Marco whispered to me.

"For what? For not speaking English?"

That kind of stopped him. We couldn't see these guys. We didn't know where they were. And we didn't know what they were doing. But that doesn't make a crime.

Then there was another sound.

Smash!

It was breaking glass. And then another sound.

Whoosh!

It was like a small bomb went off.

"Let's go!" I shouted.

Marco grabbed his cell phone, and he was right behind me. Later he told me how hard it is to punch 911 when you're running.

Downstairs, we jumped into our running shoes and grabbed our coats. By the time we got to the backyard, we could already see the flames.

"It's McNally's basement," Marco shouted.

I don't know if he was shouting at me, or at the 911 person. I didn't stop to ask. Marco was on the

cell, trying to give his address. I raced out to the front of the house.

The street was quiet. In the distance, I could hear the sirens of fire trucks. But the street was dead quiet.

Until a car started up. Suddenly the car's headlights came on. And then the car raced down the street, right past me. There were two guys in the car. I tried to look inside and see them. The driver slowed down for a second, looking at me. Then the car zoomed forward. It was going fast, too fast. Then the car turned the corner at Parker Avenue, tires squealing.

Holy ——! I thought to myself. *I just saw them. I just saw the arsonists.*

And they saw me.

The whole thing took about thirty seconds – maybe less. By then, the whole street had come alive. The cop cars and fire trucks came roaring down from Division Street. Old Mrs. McNally came out on her front porch, crying. Lights came on across the street. We were going to have lots of help in no time at all.

When I got to the backyard, I saw Marco's dad with the garden hose. It was the same hose he used to make our hockey rink in the winter. Good thing it was still hooked up. He was shooting water into Mrs. McNally's basement – just like flooding the rink. From what I could see, the fire was almost out.

"Did you see anything?" Marco asked.

But I didn't have time to answer. The fire trucks screeched to a stop out front. We could both see the flashing lights, even in back. A couple of firefighters were talking to Mrs. McNally. A couple more put on masks and air tanks, heading in the front door. And one firefighter came around back. He saw Marco's dad watering Mrs. McNally's basement.

"You know, sir," he said, "that's really our job."

Pretty nice! Thanks to us, the fire was almost out. Thanks to us, Mrs. McNally's house didn't get burned down. Thanks to us, we knew something

29

about the arsonists. But do we get a thank you? Fat chance! Instead, Marco's dad got a lecture on fire safety.

Go figure.

CHAPTER FOUR

Getting Help

We were walking back from the police station the next day. I was feeling stupid.

"You think the cops believed me?" I asked.

"Well, at least they didn't laugh," Marco replied.

"I guess," I said, kicking at a rock.

After the fire was put out, I told the cops what I'd seen and heard. The cops at the fire took me seriously. The cop took notes. He wrote down everything I said. Then he told me a detective would get back to me.

So far, so good. The detective did want to talk to

me. So Marco and I went down to the cop shop after school. That part was cool. I'd never been in a police station before. They really are like the ones on TV – all busy and messy.

But the detective thought I was a jerk. You could tell that by the look on his face. Sometimes adults just look at you like that.

"So you heard two guys talking," he began. The detective's name was Kozlow. He was reading the notes from the other cop.

"Yeah," I told him. "But not in English."

"So what language? French? Italian?"

"I don't know," I whined. "I don't think it was French." I mean, I should know a little French by now. I've been taking it since I was ten. "But I don't know other languages."

"Did it sound like this?" he said. Then Kozlow said something I didn't get.

"Kind of."

"That was Polish," he told me. "So these two guys were talking Polish?"

"Something like that. Or maybe Russian. Can you say something in Russian?"

He shot me a look. Again, he thought I was a jerk.

Kozlow changed the subject. "So you ran out in front and saw a car," he said.

"Yeah."

"Did you see the guys get in the car?"

"No."

"What kind of car was it?"

"I don't know. It was dark. Nothing special." I kept trying to picture the car, but nothing came to mind. If it were a Porsche or a BMW, I would know. But it wasn't. It was just a dull car, like a Ford or a Chevy.

"And you didn't see the license plate," Kozlow said. He was reading the other cop's notes.

"It was dark," I said.

"Most cars, the license plate is lit up," Kozlow said.

"Yeah, well, I didn't see it. Or if I saw it, I didn't get it. I mean, there was a lot going on."

"Right," Kozlow grunted. And then we went over all that again.

I think Marco and I spent a good hour with Kozlow. He kept asking questions that had no answers. Or questions I couldn't answer. Yeah, it was stupid not to get the license plate. But maybe the guys had taken the plates off. Maybe it was a stolen car. How was I supposed to know?

Then Kozlow began asking stupid questions. Why was I at Marco's house? Did we have any problems with Mrs. McNally next door? Did we ever play around with matches when we were kids?

So maybe that's why I felt stupid when we left. We'd told the truth. We'd told Kozlow everything we knew. But it felt like we were getting nowhere.

"You know what I don't like?" Marco said. We were almost back at his house.

"What?"

"The way Kozlow looked at us. It wasn't as if we were trying to help. It was as if we were suspects."

Then it all made sense – all the stupid questions. Kozlow thought we were a couple of fire-crazy kids. He thought *we* were the arsonists!

"Sh——!" I swore. "I'm not a suspect," I said, my voice rising. "I'm a victim!"

"You know, Nick," my friend said, "I think we need some help. And I think I know just the person who might do it."

Marco didn't tell me who the help would be until after dinner. And even then I didn't believe him. "Your cousin," I said. "A girl."

"A *smart* girl," Marco snapped back. "And we could use some brains on this. Unless you've suddenly had a brain transplant, Nick. In which case, I haven't noticed."

"She goes to City Arts," I mumbled.

"So? She's also a computer geek. What's the big deal?"

"Nothing. No big deal."

So we walked to one of those high-rises south of Division. Marco's cousin was up on the 11th floor. The building wasn't the greatest, but it was pretty nice. It was the kind of place with fancy furniture and fake plants in the lobby.

We knocked at 1103 and heard three or four locks click open on the other side of the door. Rosa's family didn't take chances, I guess.

"Hey, Marco," said the girl.

"Hey, Rosa," my friend replied. "This is my buddy Nick. He got burned out of 102 Amelia."

"Sorry about your house," Rosa replied.

I was a bit tongue-tied. Marco told me that his cousin was smart. What he didn't tell me was that Rosa was hot. I mean, she wasn't beautiful, but kind of striking. Now that's an old word, but it kind of works. And she sure was sexy.

"Stop drooling, Nick," Marco told me. He gave me a punch in the arm, too. "We're here to solve a crime, not hustle a girl."

"Uh, right," I replied.

And Rosa really did have brains. She had done some snooping around after Marco called her. She checked the newspaper stories online. Then she pulled up the fire department website to find out where and when the fires took place. Then she printed out a Google image of our part of the Edge. It was cool. You could see each house, each garage. You could even see the black spots where a couple of houses had burned down.

"So I put numbers on where the fires took place," Rosa explained. There they were, one to six. My house was number five. The place next to Marco's was number six. "Six houses in two months," Rosa went on. "That's no accident."

"Even the cops know that," I said.

"So do you see a pattern?" Rosa asked.

The three of us stared down at the map and the numbers. I kept looking for some order to this – back and forth, up and down, a circle. But there was nothing.

"Me neither," Rosa sighed. "It's like random.

These guys could hit any house next. There's no way of knowing."

We sat back in the living room, no better off than before. Rosa went to get a couple of Cokes, then went back to her computer.

"I looked up arson on the 'net," she said. "It's easy to figure out if a fire is arson or not. The fire marshal looks for small amounts of the fire starter. He can do tests for that, even months after the fire. There's even pictures of how they do the tests," she said, flipping her computer around to show us.

"How does this help us?" I asked.

"It doesn't," Rosa told us. "Even if the cops know it's arson, it's really hard to prove who did it. They almost have to catch the guys in the act."

"Great," I sighed.

"But I did come across one thing that might help," she said. Then she paused, looking at the two of us. "Motive." One word – that was it.

"Motive?" I asked.

"It means, why did somebody do it," Marco told me.

"I know that," I snapped back. He was making me look like a fool in front of this girl. "How stupid do you think I am?"

Marco and I glared at each other.

"If you two are finished," Rosa broke in, "I'll explain." That was enough to shut us up. "There are a couple common motives for arson," she said. "One is insurance. People burn down their own houses for insurance money."

"Well, that wouldn't work for my house," I said. "We didn't have insurance. All the stuff we had went up in the fire."

Rosa still looked at me. "What about the man downstairs, the owner?"

"Mr. Rouse didn't have any money. He even had trouble paying his taxes. I don't think he had insurance. Besides, he was an old guy. He was *born* in that house. Nobody would burn down the place they were born."

"What about the place next to you?" she asked Marco.

"Same thing," Marco replied. "Mrs. McNally is, like, a hundred years old. You think an old lady would pay somebody to burn down her own house?"

"Okay, so scratch motive number one. It's not insurance," Rosa replied.

"What's motive number two?"

"A pyromaniac," she said. "A crazy guy who starts fires," Rosa explained. "See, the cops think *you're* the pyromaniac."

"Oh, swell," I groaned.

"But Nick heard *two* guys talking," Marco jumped in. "No way there could be two crazy guys in the same neighborhood. I mean, that's too weird."

"So motive two is unlikely," Rosa said. "Then there's motive number three – shakedown. A protection racket. I read that gangs are getting into this."

"So a gang guy would ask for protection money. Pay up or we'll burn down your house," Marco explained.

"That's how it works," Rosa told him.

"I can't picture it," I told them. "Can you see old Mrs. McNally even talking to a gangsta? Or old Mr. Rouse? Maybe it would work in the ghetto, but not in the Edge."

There was a silence after that. The truth is, half the Edge was ghetto. That included the highrise we were in right now.

"That's pretty much what I thought. But then I looked at the map and got one more idea. Look at these two blocks where all the fires have been. Then look up north, here. What's going on?"

"Condos," I said. "They're building condos."

"And here to the west?"

"More condos. It's where the old hospital used to be."

"But these two blocks of houses kind of stand in the way, don't they?" Rosa said. "Two blocks of lousy

42

old houses, not worth all that much. But with lots of old people who won't sell for any price."

"But they might sell if they were scared," I said. "And they'd sell cheap."

Suddenly, the three of us were smiling. We didn't have a *who* yet, but we had come up with a *why*.

CHAPTER FIVE

Grunt work is what they call it. Grunt work is the dull, dirty work you do to get a job done. Boring work. For the next couple of days, the three of us did grunt work. We knew *why* the Edge was burning; we needed to find out who was behind it.

Marco began with his parents.

"Dad, Mom," he began, "I was wondering. Has anybody come by trying to buy the house?"

"Wish somebody would," grumbled Marco's

dad. "Old houses like this always need work. Really could use a new furnace."

His mom looked at Marco with concern. "Are you unhappy here?" she asked. "We've never really thought about moving. We always thought —"

Marco cut her off. "No, I don't *want* to move. But we think some real estate guy might be behind all the fires."

"That's a good one." Marco's dad laughed.

"So we're checking it out," Marco went on. "And I thought I'd begin right here. You know how real estate guys sometimes knock on the door. Do you remember any of them? Were any of them kind of pushy?"

"Did any of them sound Polish or Russian?" I threw in.

Both Marco's parents looked at us like we were nuts.

"Kids, I think you should let the police handle this. Some crazy guy is setting these fires, but they'll catch him," said Marco's mom.

"It's not . . . ," I began, but then caught myself. *What's the use?* I thought. The cops didn't believe us. Neither would Marco's parents.

That night, we talked about it. I bounced on the blow-up mattress. Marco sat up in his bed. We tried to figure out if *all* parents were useless, or just *some* parents. It was a long talk, and we never really finished it. Marco just fell asleep and began snoring. I turned over and played an old video game. Then it was morning.

Sometimes your brain works better in the morning. I woke up with an idea – I'd call Mr. Rouse. Since we didn't own our old house, nobody could ask us to sell it. But Mr. Rouse did own the house, and he'd lived on the first floor. All sorts of real estate guys must have come by.

So I phoned my mom, and she had his number. Mr. Rouse had gone off to live with a nephew until he could move somewhere. So I punched the numbers, asked for Mr. Rouse, then shouted into the cell phone.

"Mr. Rouse," I shouted. "Can you hear me?"

"Just a minute," he sputtered. "Got to fix this dang hearing aid."

I knew all about the hearing aid. Mr. Rouse was always turning it up or down. When he turned it up, sometimes it shrieked so loudly that I could hear it. When he turned it down, he was deaf as a doughnut. The old guy never got it quite right.

"It's Nick," I shouted.

"Who's that?"

"Nick! From the old house. Upstairs."

"Oh, right. Nick. Little Nick," he said. That's what he called me from when I was about two years old. "Nice to hear from you. How's your mother?"

"Good," I said. "But I've got a question for you."

"Okay, go for it," he said.

"Do you remember any real estate guys trying to buy your house? I mean, in the last year or so."

"Sure, lots of 'em," he said. "That was a beautiful house, Little Nick. I could have made a pretty penny if I had sold that place, back before the fire."

Really, it was not a beautiful house. Maybe fifty years ago, when Mr. Rouse was a young man, but not when I lived in it. It think old guys live in the past a lot. Or maybe Mr. Rouse was as blind as he was deaf.

"Do you remember any of those guys?" I asked. "Any of them talk with an accent, maybe Polish or Russian?"

"Can't say, Little Nick," he replied. "You know my hearing's not so good."

"Really?" I said, trying to sound surprised.

"Yup, can't hear worth a dang. And those real estate guys, never gave them the time of day. I was going to live in that house until my dying day. Hah! Let that be a lesson to you, Little Nick."

I wasn't sure what the lesson was, but I didn't give up. "So do you remember any names, or did you keep any record?"

"Sure," he said.

My eyes brightened up. Marco was listening and he thought I was getting somewhere.

"Those real estate guys always leave a card," Mr. Rouse went on. "And I kept all those cards. Must have been fifty of 'em. I'd put 'em in that old desk in the front hall. You remember it, don't you? My mother bought that desk back in '33 or '34. Set her back a pretty penny, it did."

Then I got this sinking feeling. I knew what was coming.

"Too bad about that desk. Nothing left of it. Nothing left of the whole dang house except the walls." Then there was a funny noise from his end of the line. I couldn't be sure, but I think Mr. Rouse was crying.

"Right," I said. "Well, sorry to bother you."

"Not a bother, Little Nick," he said, sniffling. "You call any time, y'hear."

"Yes, sir."

"Any time at all."

I pushed the end button and that was that. Once again, I felt stupid. Actually, I felt worse because I made old Mr. Rouse cry. He was a nice old man, and he'd grown up in that old house. If the fire was bad for me, it must have been awful for him.

So I looked up at Marco and shrugged. A couple of dead ends. We'd been doing spade work and hit rocks just below the surface.

Then we got the same idea at the same time. "Mrs. McNally!" we said in one voice.

In no time, we were over at her house. It took Mrs. McNally a while to get to the door, but she was happy to see us both.

"You boys saved my house," she said cheerfully. "You and your father. And to think of all those times I made a fuss about that hockey rink back there. Well, I am sorry. You two boys can play hockey as much as you want."

"Actually, we're not here to talk about hockey," Marco said. Then he went on to ask the question about real estate guys.

This time, we struck the jackpot.

"Don't much talk to those people," Mrs. McNally said. "But I do try to be polite. I always smile when

they tell me how much this house is worth . . . and I take their card. It's the polite thing to do, even if some of them are a bit rude. I do try —"

Marco cut her off. "Do you keep the cards, Mrs. McNally?"

"Well, of course," she said. "Never throw anything out. Let me just see here . . ."

It took ten minutes of searching. Mrs. McNally did not just save business cards. She saved letters, newspaper, magazines, books, old coins, TV Guides and flyers from Pizza Pizza. "Just in case," she said.

But there they were – over a hundred business cards from real estate guys. And bonus! Mrs. McNally had written a date on each card. It was a gold mine.

That night, we got together with Rosa. I've got to say, she was looking good. A tight top, some tight jeans, and maybe even some eye makeup. I know I wasn't supposed to stare, but I did.

Marco just looked at me and shook his head. "Hopeless," I heard him groan.

"So what have you guys been up to?" Rosa asked.

"We've been doing grunt work," Marco told her. "We've been digging for clues." Then we explained what we did. Marco pulled out a list of all the real estate guys who'd left a card with Mrs. McNally. There were two companies that kept coming up, over and over. The cards said Re-Nu Real Estate and Bender Builders.

"Not bad," Rosa said. "But that was a lot less work than what I did."

We both stared at her.

"What did you do?" I asked.

"Went down to City Hall," she told us. "They have a computer that tells you who owns each house in town. It also tells you how much a house is worth and what the taxes are. Want to know what your house is worth, Marco?"

"Nah. Not really."

"I'll tell you anyhow. $280,000."

"But my house is junky," he said.

"Yeah, but the land that it sits on is worth real money."

Both Marco and I began scratching our heads. What did this have to do with arson?

"Anyhow, guess who owns about ten houses in those two blocks."

We both looked blank.

"C'mon, guys. Think. It's a company . . . starts with an R . . ."

Then I got it. "Re-Nu Real Estate."

"Ta-dah!" she said.

So then we all sat there, kind of stunned. We think we knew the *why* behind the arson. Now maybe we had the *who*. Only one question was left.

What should we do next?

CHAPTER SIX

Face to Face

I woke up in the middle of the night with an answer. It was enough to make me sit up in the blow-up bed.

"You hear something?" Marco said.

Neither one of us could sleep all that well. It's hard to sleep when you're half-listening to sounds outside the house. After all, the arsonists had tried once to burn down Mrs. McNally's house. They might try again.

"Nah," I told him. "I had an idea."

"Yeah?"

"I think we should go visit Re-Nu Real Estate. They've got to have an office. We can tell them to stop the arson or we'll go to the cops."

"Nick, I think you watch too much TV," Marco replied.

"Yeah?"

"For one thing, real bad guys don't just stop when they get a warning. I mean, the arsonists are ready to kill somebody to get hold of a house. They're not going to stop just because we tell them to. For another thing, they'll just say we're crazy. I mean, the cops don't believe us. Why should some business guys believe us?"

"Because . . . uh, because they're guilty?"

"Go back to sleep, Nick. Maybe your brain will work better with some sleep."

My brain didn't work any better that morning. In fact, neither Marco nor I could come up with a better idea. Marco did phone Det. Kozlow with what we had found, but Kozlow was out. Marco could only leave a phone message. That meant it was all up to us. Maybe we wouldn't confront the real estate guys, but we could snoop around.

So that day we took the subway downtown. It takes a good half hour to get downtown from the Edge. Right away, Marco and I knew we didn't belong down here. All these guys in suits, and the two of us in jeans. Still, we kept going. I wasn't sure what I was going to say to the guys at Re-Nu, but we had to do something. It was only a matter of time, really. Houses in the Edge would keep burning; Re-Nu would keep buying those that were left. Then – condo city.

Re-Nu Real Estate was up on the 14th floor of a big glass building. The place looked pretty classy down in the lobby. But the 14th floor had a lot of small offices. One of them had the sign: Re-Nu Real Estate. We stopped outside it.

"You sure you want to snoop around here?" Marco asked.

"Got a better idea?" I replied. "We'll just go in and look around. Maybe there'll be a clue."

"Maybe we'll hear the Russian guys," Marco said.

"You never know." Then I turned the handle and the two of us walked in.

The Re-Nu office was pretty small. There was a woman at a desk out front, then two offices at the back. The offices at the back must have had the windows. Out in front, it was pretty dark.

"How can I help you?" asked the woman. She was my mom's age but trying to look younger. Dyed hair, tight sweater, all that. The kind of things old women do to pretend they're still twenty.

"We were . . . uh . . . ," Marco began. I don't think either one of us expected to *talk* to somebody. We were just looking for clues.

"Uh, is this Re-Nu Real Estate?" A pretty stupid question, since there was a sign on the door. Still, it bought me some time to think.

"Yes, what can we do for you?" the woman asked.

"Well, uh, I hear that you people are buying houses . . . in Edgemont." At least that made sense.

"Yes, I think we're planning a development there," she replied. She batted her eyelashes at me. They were fake. I had a hunch that a lot of her was fake. "Do you have a house to sell . . . or perhaps your parents do?"

"Yes," I lied. This was good. Now I had some reason to be here. "My parents might sell. Maybe I could talk to . . . uh . . . ," I left it blank. I had no idea who was behind her, in the two offices.

"Mr. Liddell," she said, filling the blank. "And whom should I say is waiting?"

So I could have made up a name, couldn't I? I could have refused to say anything. I could have kept my mouth shut. But no, I just blurted it out.

"Nick Messina," I told her. "And this is my friend Marco — "

But Marco was smart enough to cut me off. He gave me a kick in the leg before I could finish. So Mrs. Fake Eyelashes never got his last name.

"Please have a seat. Mr. Liddell will see you shortly."

We sat. I picked up a magazine and pretended to read. I kept looking around for a clue, but there was nothing. It was just an office. Just a stupid office.

We sat out there for maybe ten minutes. The office was pretty quiet. The woman at the desk played some kind of mellow rock music, but that was all. The phone didn't ring. Nobody came in.

Then the door to one inner office opened up. Out came a tall guy with slicked back hair. He was wearing a suit, but you could see that he was a big guy – big shoulders, big arms. He could have been a boxer or a wrestler.

"How can I help you gentlemen?" he asked. He had a pretty deep voice, but it wasn't Russian or Polish.

"Could we talk inside your office?" I asked.

That was no problem. We went inside the office, sat down on two modern chairs, and looked at the view outside through big windows.

"So you live in Edgemont?" he began.

I wondered if I should try to act like a tough guy. On TV, that always seems to work. But "tough guy" wasn't one of my better acts. I ended up just being me.

"Yeah," I said. "We both do."

"Your parents thinking of selling their houses?"

"Yes, they might be," I lied. "We hear that your company is buying a lot of houses in the Edge."

"When we can," he said. He leaned back in his chair, cool as could be. "Lots of old folks out there. It could take a long time to get the land we need."

"Unless the houses burn down," Marco threw in.

Liddell didn't even blink. "True," he replied. "Lots of fires out in that neighborhood. Some crazy guy . . . that's what the papers say."

"It's not a crazy guy," I replied, "it's arson." Now I was getting as pushy as Marco. "Maybe somebody had a reason to set those fires."

"Oh, so you two know something about this?" He looked at me hard, maybe for the first time.

"Maybe we do," I said, "and maybe we don't." Was that good, or what? I felt like I should be on CSI.

"So what can I do for you . . . exactly?" Liddell asked. Somehow his tone wasn't friendly anymore. Liddell stared at us; we stared at him. There was a fan some place, humming. Outside, we could hear EZ Rock from the waiting room.

So far we had come up with nothing. I decided to push a little harder.

"We wondered what you know about the fires," I said. "We kind of wondered something. How come there are no fires in the houses that you guys own?"

"Beats me," Liddell replied. "I thought you were here about your parents' house. But now it sounds like you kids are trying to imply something."

I cut him off. "We're just asking questions."

Liddell stood up. He towered over us. "Well, I'm finished giving answers, kid. I don't like where this is going. We're a well-known company, kids. We buy

63

houses at a fair price. We don't play around with arson, and we don't break the law."

"Do you have anyone Polish or Russian who works for you?"

Then Liddell got really mad. "All right, out of my office," he said. His voice got loud and angry. "This is stupid. Get out of here, both of you!"

By now, he was moving around his desk. Liddell was as big as the two of us, combined. I had a hunch he might pick us both up and throw us out the door.

But Marco and I were on our feet, moving fast. I wasn't sure about Marco, but I was scared. I didn't want to get hit by this guy. He could wallop me like a freight train.

We got to the waiting room just as the door to the hall opened up. Two guys came in, talking to each other. They weren't speaking English.

Then we had one of those slow-motion moments. All in all, it lasted maybe five seconds. We came out to the waiting room. The two guys came in from the hallway. Liddell came out behind us. Mrs. Fake Eyelashes at the desk looked up. All that was fine.

But as we passed the two guys, one of them stopped. He looked at me – really looked hard at me – and stopped dead. I looked back and had the funny feeling I'd seen him before. So we exchanged a look, for maybe a second or two. It was creepy.

Then Marco grabbed me. He was already at the door, ready to go. Marco pulled my arm and yanked, hard, to get me out of there. I followed him, pulling the door closed.

"Move it," Marco shouted. "Take the stairs. We're not waiting for the elevator, Nick. We're getting out of here, like fast."

CHAPTER SEVEN

Okay, so nobody chased us down the stairs. There were no guys waiting down in the lobby to jump us. It wasn't like a movie. It was all kind of . . . stupid.

"You think those Re-Nu guys are guilty?" Marco asked. We were on the subway, at rush hour. That meant we were standing and holding onto a strap.

"Yeah, for sure."

"Because of the Russian guys," he said.

"Yeah. That was the tip off. I knew the one guy, and he knew me. But how do you know they're Russian?"

"I watch too much TV," he sighed.

So what then? We had clues, lots of them. We had motive. We could even pick out the Russian guys who set the fire. But I knew that nobody would believe us. I knew that Kozlow would laugh it all off.

So we went over to Rosa's place. If anybody could think this through, she could. Besides, I was looking for some excuse to see her again. Maybe Marco didn't think she was a hottie, but I did.

It was Marco who told her all about Re-Nu and the Russians.

She sighed. "Pretty dumb, *ciuuco*," she said.

"The Russian guys?" I asked.

"No, you two," Rosa declared. "What were you trying to prove by going there? Did you think the guy would just confess? I mean, how much TV do you watch?"

Both Marco and I turned red in the face. Rosa was right, of course. We had gone over there with no plan. And now we had nothing to show for it. Actually, it was worse than nothing.

"And now all those Re-Nu guys know about you, Nick," she went on. "Maybe you should paint a target on your back. Wear a sign that says 'shoot me,' or something like that."

"C'mon," I said. "We're not that dumb. We never told them our names . . . ," I began. And then I groaned. Yeah, I did give Ms. Fake Eyelashes my name.

Marco shot me a look.

Rosa just shook her head. "So now the Russians know who you are. If we're right about these guys, you're in real danger, Nick."

Then I had a brainwave. "But they don't know where I live," I said. "I mean, they can look me up, but my house burned down. So how are they going to find me, eh? How are they going to know I'm at Marco's house?"

"Nick's right," Marco joined in. "And I never told them my name."

"Well, at least you did one smart thing," Rosa declared. "But do me a favor, Nick. On the way home from school, keep your eyes open for the two Russian guys. I have a hunch they'll be keeping an eye out for you."

"Yeah, yeah."

"And you better go see Det. Kozlow. Make sure he knows all this before . . . uh, before anything else happens."

So we left another long message for Kozlow. As if he really cared. And then we went down for dinner with Marco's parents. They were looking pretty grim.

"What's the matter?" Marco asked.

"Your great-aunt Maria died," replied his mom.

"Who?"

"Your grandma's sister," she snapped back. "You know, the lady who always gave you books when you were little."

"Uh, right," Marco replied. I had a hunch Marco didn't remember his great-aunt at all.

That's when Marco's dad gave us the news. "So we're driving to Boston for the funeral," he said. "You could come, I suppose, but where would Nick stay?"

"That's okay, Dad," Marco said quickly. "I mean, I only met Aunt Maria once or twice . . . and then there's school."

Marco gave them a nice smile. Actually, it was a fake smile. Marco didn't worry about school, and he didn't care much about his great-aunt. But a weekend of full-time Wii was too good to pass up.

And I had an even better idea. I ran it by Marco after dinner.

"You think Rosa would go out with me?"

"What?" Marco asked. "She thinks you're an idiot."

"Yeah, but I'm a cute idiot," I said. "And she's a hottie."

Marco shook his head. He went back to doing homework. Can you imagine that? He actually went back to homework.

"Okay, I've got a better idea," I said.

Marco groaned.

"I bet Rosa has a hot friend. And I bet that hot friend would love to go out with you."

"What hot friend?" he asked. Now I had his interest.

"I don't know. Hot girls always hang around with other hot girls. Rosa's a dancer. Maybe she'll come up with a dancer for you." I kept smiling at him. "You know how hot dancers can be." I left that idea sitting in his brain for a couple seconds. "So maybe we go out to a movie on Friday. Then, if it works out, we have the house to ourselves all weekend. You get my meaning?"

"You're dreaming," Marco said.

"Yeah, maybe I am," I told him. "But it's worth a try."

Marco grunted. Then he complained. Then he said it would never work. But after a couple of minutes he gave in . . . so long as I made the phone call.

I wish I could report that I was real cool when I phoned Rosa. I wish I could say that I was so smooth she was panting into her cell phone. But neither was true. I was pretty nervous when I called. My voice got all high and shaky. I was pretty dumb when I started talking to her, and then I got worse when I asked the question. "Marco and I were wondering about Friday night."

"Wondering what?" she asked.

"Well . . . uh . . . you know, we were thinking of a movie . . . and . . . uh . . ." My hand was sweating.

"Which movie?"

"I . . . uh . . . a movie movie, you know?"

Maybe Marco was right. Maybe I was an idiot. Maybe this was all just stupid. Maybe Rosa would shoot me down in flames.

But that didn't happen. Rosa saved the whole thing. She even seemed to like the idea of going out with me . . . or at least with Marco and me. There was some dance movie she wanted to see. And she had a friend, some girl named Lee, who might be

perfect for Marco. And maybe we could all meet at the Pinecrest at nine o'clock.

It was all that simple. I was smiling when I hung up the phone.

"How'd you do?" Marco asked when I got back to the basement.

"We're set," I said. "Nine o'clock on Friday. She's got some hot dancer friend for you. A blonde."

Marco gave me a nod. I took it as a nod of respect.

"Pretty smooth, Nick," he said.

"Yeah," I agreed, grinning from ear to ear. "I can be pretty smooth with women."

CHAPTER EIGHT

Night Visitors

I wasn't stupid the rest of that week. Really I wasn't.
I hadn't forgotten about the Russian guys. I knew
they were looking for me. So I kept my hoodie up
when I walked to school. And Marco kept his eyes
open for anyone looking for us.

But there were no guys lurking in cars. No guys
were hanging out on the street, waiting. It was like
that whole scene at Re-Nu Real Estate had never
happened.

Even Det. Kozlow laughed it off. "Kid, you can't

just talk to business guys like that. No wonder that Liddell guy got angry. You two kids should leave the police work to us. It's safer that way."

Yeah, yeah.

Besides, I had other stuff on my mind. I was going out with a hot girl on Friday night. That meant I needed some decent clothes. And that meant a trip to Goodwill and using up the last of my Red Cross money.

It's funny how my life at Marco's place had come to seem like normal. It was as if I'd always shared a bedroom with him. As if we'd always been like brothers. As if his parents were really my parents. Maybe that's why I got careless. Maybe it was all too easy.

Marco's parents took off early Friday. We had a little party when we got home: pizza and a beer from Marco's dad's supply. He wouldn't miss just two beers . . . or four, as it turned out. Then we went downstairs to play *Wii Boxing* for a while. We had time to kill before meeting the girls at nine o'clock.

We were right in the middle of a game when there was a noise upstairs.

"You hear something?" Marco asked.

"Yeah. Me breathing hard."

"I mean, upstairs."

"Nah, nothing," I replied, punching his guy about five times.

"Hey, no fair. New game!"

So then we tried *Dance Dance Revolution*. Marco said that I'd better learn to dance now that I was hustling girls. I didn't bother to laugh. DDR was kind of fun, but hard work. I never got past the basic stage, and I looked pretty stupid even at that. The Wii kept saying, "Try harder" while the crowd noise kept booing me. It was hard work, for a game. In no time, I'd worked up a sweat.

"Okay, shower time," I said. "I'm first."

"You want to smell nice for Rosa?"

"I just don't want to smell like a dirty undershirt," I snapped back. "I suggest the same for you, stinko."

"Hey, I don't sweat like you, Nick. But I'm next. Leave me some hot water."

Marco always made fun of my long showers. But what's the big deal? Turn the water on, sing a song or two, soap up, get wet. To me, a shower is the nicest part of the day. I might as well make it last.

So I was feeling pretty good when I bopped up the stairs. I was thinking about going to the movies with Rosa. And I was thinking about what we might do after the movies. And I was wondering what I'd sing in the shower.

But I didn't get that far.

I was walking by the kitchen when they grabbed me. I tried to open my mouth and cry out, but they stuck something in it. Then a sack was pulled over my head. In two seconds, I was trapped. I couldn't move. I felt like I couldn't breathe.

"Keep your mouth shut," one guy whispered. He had an accent – Russian or Polish.

I could feel a knife poking into my back. That,

and the gag in my mouth, made it simple. I shut up. I didn't even struggle.

But my brain kept working. There were two of them, one of me. They had at least one knife. I had nothing but a sack over my head. What could I do?

Down in the basement, I heard Marco playing Wii boxing. He was losing. The Wii was winning. I could tell from the crowd noises. In ten minutes or so, he'd come upstairs. Then these guys would have both of us. What could I do before then? What signal could I make?

Marco's cell phone rang. He paused the game and answered.

"Hey, Rosa," he began. I could hear his voice coming up from the basement. "Chilling." She must have asked what he was doing.

"Yeah, Nick is up taking a shower. He's got the hots for you, cuz. I think he wants to smell pretty . . . just for you."

I couldn't hear Rosa groan, but I had a hunch she did.

"Yeah, I've got to take a shower too. Tell me, is this dancer chick hot?" There was a pause. "Hey, don't call me a pig. I was just asking."

This was so weird. My buddy was downstairs, goofing around on the phone. I was upstairs with a sack over my head and a knife against my back.

"Yeah. See you soon. Bye." I could picture Marco pushing the end button.

A lost chance. If I could have come up with a signal, while he was on the phone . . . but no, I couldn't. I was scared. I was having a hard time breathing. And I had a hunch I was going to die.

Then Marco shouted upstairs. "Nick, you going to start that shower or what?"

Of course. Down in the basement, he could hear water running up the pipes. He knew I wasn't in the shower.

"Nick, we've got to get going," he shouted.

I said nothing. I couldn't even grunt. There was a something in my mouth and a knife at my back.

"You jerk!" he yelled. "Get in that shower, fast, or you go out stinky. Now move."

I heard him coming up the stairs.

"Nick," he called up to me. "We've got to . . . ," he stopped. Marco had reached the top of the stairs. He saw me. He saw the two guys.

"Holy ——" he swore.

I heard him run down the stairs. Then one of the guys left me and ran after him.

I figured I had maybe five seconds. I knew Marco was running for his phone. I knew the Russian guy would be on him in no time. I knew the guy who held me was my size, maybe smaller. But my arms and hands were trapped in the sack. What could I do?

Use your legs, stupid, I told myself.

I tried to figure where the guy was. Then I turned, fast as I could. The knife blade sliced into me, but still I turned. When I was all the way around – when I thought he was in front of me – I rammed my knee into his crotch.

"F——," he swore.

I got him. I got him where it hurts. But now what? I tried to lift the sack over my head so I could see. I tried to get free.

And that's when a fist slammed into my face.

When I came to, I was on the kitchen floor. My hands and feet were tied together. Another rope was tied to the table so I couldn't move.

Marco was on the other side of the room. He was tied up, as I was, but he was still out cold. There was blood dripping from his mouth, and his forehead was already turning black and blue.

"You killed him. You killed my best friend."

I heard a laugh from behind me.

"Not yet, kiddo," said a voice. The accent was thick.

I tried to twist my head, but I couldn't see the guy. Downstairs, I could hear somebody moving around. It sounded like he was ripping up newspapers.

"Make good fire, eh?" the one guy yelled.

The voice in the basement answered. It was something in Russian, but it sounded like "shut up."

I couldn't see either of them. I couldn't move my hands or feet. And my head was still pounding like I'd been hit with a big hammer. But I had to do something. If I just lay there, I knew they'd kill us both.

"You can't do this," I said. "It's murder." I waited, but the guys said nothing. I wondered if they knew the word *murder*. "If you kill us, the cops will come after you. It's not like burning a house. If you kill someone, the cops will find you."

I tried to speak slowly, but my voice was squeaky.

"No murder," said the one guy. "Accident."

Now I could make sense of it. They had us tied down. Then they'd start a fire in the basement. The fire would work its way upstairs and we'd be cooked. After the whole house was burned up, how would anyone know we had been tied up? How would they know we didn't start the fire ourselves?

"Listen," I begged. "Nobody has to know about this. Let us go and we won't tell the police. We won't tell anybody."

The one guy told me to shut up, but I didn't.

"You can't do this," I cried. I really was crying, not just saying it. "We're just kids. We never hurt you."

"You see my face, kiddo," the guy replied. Then he crossed over the room and knelt down in front of me. "You see it again, now," he said. He pushed his face right in front of mine. "But you never see it again, kiddo. Never see any face again."

I wanted to hit him. I wanted to spit at him. I wanted to do something, but I was trapped by the ropes.

The guy got up, and then the house phone rang. The guy in front of me got up and found the phone. For a second, I thought he might answer it. But no, he just ripped it from the wall.

The guy in the basement came upstairs. Again

the two guys said something in Russian. The next thing I knew, one of them went outside. I guess he had to get something from the car.

I just lay on the floor. If I could just get out of the ropes, I thought, I might have a chance. There was only the one guy, and one of me. If I could get my hands free . . . but these two knew what they were doing. I couldn't pull my hands free. I couldn't pull on the knots. I couldn't even turn over to see what was going on.

In a few minutes, the other guy came back. He must have brought something with him. He walked downstairs and I heard some kind of splashing. Soon the house smelled like gasoline.

"You don't want to do this," I said. *Keep talking*, I told myself. *It's your only hope.* "You ever have kids? Can you imagine somebody doing this to your kids? Why don't you think about this a little? I don't know who you are. I've got nothing to tell the cops. Nothing."

From across the room, Marco groaned. I looked

over and saw him open his eyes. I wasn't sure how much he could see. He seemed kind of sick.

"Better your friend not wake up," said the one guy. He went over and kicked Marco in the gut. My friend grunted, then went out cold again.

"Is better for him," said the guy. "You," he said to me, "you see too much. You make all this to happen." Then he bent down close to my face. "You, kiddo, will see the fire come to you. You will see your body burn!"

He laughed, then stepped back. He yelled something in Russian to the guy downstairs. That guy yelled something back. There was more movement, then the downstairs guy came up to the kitchen.

I heard one of them strike a match. Nothing happened right away. There must have been some kind of fuse going down the stairs. But after twenty seconds, I heard a *whoosh*. I could smell smoke coming up the stairs.

And I knew I was going to die.

CHAPTER NINE

Stood Up

Rosa and her friend Lee were standing outside the Pinecrest Mall. Inside was the 8-plex of movie screens. Outside, where they stood, it was cold.

"They'll be here," Rosa said. She stamped her feet on the ground. There was fresh snow.

"This cousin of yours had better be cute," Lee said.

"He is," Rosa told her. "And he's never late. I mean, Marco wouldn't just stand us up. And Nick is a decent guy, too. I think."

"Trust me," Lee sighed. "There are no decent guys. There are cute guys, hot guys and cruddy guys, but no decent guys."

"Would you cut it out," Rosa groaned.

"Okay, but my point about guys remains the same. Let's forget them and go see the movie. We've been stood up, Rosa. It's as simple as that."

Rosa looked at her watch again. It was 9:12. The guys were late. Inside, the movie was almost ready to start, but the girls didn't even have tickets. All they had were cold feet from the snow. And Lee was getting angry.

"They're probably playing video games," Lee said. "They probably forgot, or got scared. I mean, who knows with guys?" Lee shook her head. From her experience, all guys were jerks. "Besides, I'm cold, Rosa. I want to go in. Let's forget those jerks and see the movie."

"Yeah, in just a second. We'll give them a second more."

"You said that ten minutes ago," Lee whined.

"You called them on your cell . . . all for nothing. The guys are losers, Rosa."

"No, they're not," Rosa repeated. "At least Marco isn't. I've known him all my life, and he's a *good* guy. He wouldn't ditch us like this unless . . ." A light went on in her brain.

"Unless what?"

"Unless they were in trouble."

"Yeah, right," Lee replied, shaking her head. "Guys always have an excuse."

"No, but this time . . . ," Rosa's voice dropped off.

Rosa could see the Division Street bus coming from the east. If the guys were in trouble, they'd need help. The bus could get them to Marco's house in ten minutes. Rosa thought about that – the movie or the bus. Then she made up her mind.

"C'mon, Lee. Let's go find the guys," she shouted. Then Rosa grabbed Lee and pulled her to the bus stop. In seconds, they were riding down Division Street.

It was crazy, Lee kept saying. Most of the time,

most guys, and it would be a simple story. They changed their minds. They couldn't care less. One guy got cold feet. They forgot. Guys are pretty awful like that.

But Marco wasn't like that. Rosa had known him all her life, and he was a straight shooter. Besides, she remembered that the Russian guy had seen Nick downtown. He had recognized Nick. There was a chance – just a chance – that both Nick and Marco could be in big trouble.

Rosa phoned Marco's cell again. No answer. Then she rang the house phone. She heard some kind of fast beeping sound. She thought it was kind of strange.

"Are you going to explain this, or what?" Lee demanded. She was sulking in her seat.

"Okay, I'll explain."

Rosa told her the story, or at least a short version of it. When she was finished, Lee asked the simple question.

"So you think they're in trouble?"

"Yeah, maybe," Rosa replied

"And what if the two of them just forgot? What if we find them playing Wii or something?"

Rosa looked at her and spoke very carefully. "Then they really are in trouble . . . because we are going to *kill* them!"

Lee's eyes grew bright, and they both gave a nervous laugh.

By then, the bus pulled up to the stop at Bendigo Street and both girls got off. It was two blocks to Marco's house. They could have walked, Rosa thought, but if the guys really were in trouble . . .

So they ran. Both Lee and Rosa were in good shape from dancing. They weren't even breathing hard when they reached the corner of Amelia. The girls could see Marco's house from the corner. They could see a dark car parked in front of the place. And they saw a guy running out of Marco's place and into the car.

"Move it!" Rosa screamed to Lee.

The two of them began running down the street

just as a second guy came out of the house. He hopped into the car as the girls got close.

"Can you see the plates?" Rosa asked

"Yeah . . . YYK something."

Then there was a flash of yellow light from the house. Both girls could both see the rest of the number.

"4476."

Then the car took off. In another second, it had zoomed way down the street. But the girls weren't watching the car anymore. They were watching flames shooting out of the basement of Marco's house.

Rosa gave Lee her purse and her cell phone. "Call 911," she yelled. "Get help."

"What are you going to do?"

"If the guys are in there," she told her. "I'm gonna try to bring them out!"

Rosa wrapped her scarf around her face and went up on the porch. She could see that the flames were still downstairs. There was white smoke pouring out the basement windows, but only white smoke.

The black smoke is the killer, she told herself. She'd read that somewhere. If you breathe black smoke, it will knock you out. And in a couple of minutes, you're dead. But white smoke isn't so bad. White smoke meant she still had time.

"Marco, Nick!" she yelled out. Then she coughed. *Don't breathe in the smoke,* she told herself. She put her hand against the door. It was still cold. The fire hadn't made it to the first floor yet.

"Marco, Nick!" she yelled again.

This time she heard coughing from inside the house. "We're . . . we're in here," she heard. "In the kitchen." It was Nick's voice, but it was faint. And then he started coughing.

Rosa turned to look at Lee. How much time did they have?

"The fire department is coming," Lee told her.

In a couple minutes, they'd be at the house. Rosa could wait for them. She could pray that the firefighters would show up before the whole house went up in flames.

But her cousin Marco was inside that house. So was his friend Nick. Somehow the guys were trapped, they couldn't get out. Even now, they couldn't breathe. In a couple of minutes, they could be dead.

So Rosa made up her mind right there. "The guys are inside," she told Lee. "You stay here. I'm going in to get them."

"Rosa . . . ," Lee called out, but Rosa wasn't listening.

Rosa took one more deep breath of air, held the scarf to her face, and pushed open the door.

Smoke poured out at her as she went inside the house. On top, the smoke was white. At her feet, the smoke was now black.

Down below, Rosa could see the flames. They were coming up the stairs from the basement. Soon the flames would reach the first floor, and then the whole house would go up. In seconds, the whole place could be in flames.

"I'm coming," Rosa shouted. She could barely see ahead of her, but she knew Marco's house. She knew how to find the kitchen, even walking blind. In seconds, she felt the fridge near the kitchen door. In the middle of the room, on the floor, she saw two shapes. It was all so hazy, so smoky, but she knew the shapes had to be Nick and Marco.

"C'mon," she shouted. "Let's get out of there!"

Neither of them moved.

Rosa's eyes were full of tears. She kept walking forward, barely able to see. She couldn't speak any more — she needed all the air in her lungs. So she walked forward until her feet hit something — or somebody.

Rosa bent down. It was Nick, but he was out cold. She tried to pull his arm, to pull him up, but his arm wouldn't move. Then she felt the rope, and it all made sense.

A knife, she said to herself. *I need a knife.*

She tried to remember where Marco's parents kept the knives. This was the kitchen – one of the drawers would have a knife. She walked over to the sink and pulled open the first drawer. Towels. Then a second drawer. Silverware. She bent down close and found what she wanted. A steak knife.

In no time, she was back down beside Nick. She took the knife and began cutting the rope. Soon his arm was free. Then she found another rope on his leg. She cut at that, working against time, working against the smoke. At last, Nick was free.

Get up! she said in her mind. *Don't just die on me like this. Get up!*

But Nick did nothing. He was a dead weight in her arms. She didn't have the strength left to drag him out.

Rosa wanted to cry, or swear, or something. But her air was running out.

Maybe I can get Marco out, she said to herself.

But the smoke was so thick Rosa couldn't see

her own hands. She couldn't see where Marco was. All she could see were the flames in the front hall.

The fire had burned its way upstairs. The flames were just outside in the hall. The smoke now was all thick and black. It was impossible to breathe. It was impossible to save Nick and Marco. Maybe there was time to save herself. If she could just get out the back door . . . if she could just find the back door . . .

But she felt so tired. She felt like she couldn't move at all. She felt like she just wanted to lie down on the floor and sleep. Just lie down and sleep . . . forever.

CHAPTER TEN

Maybe a Hero

When I opened my eyes, I couldn't really see. I was in some kind of room, with a machine going beep-beep-beep. It sounded like a fire alarm, but quiet.

"What!" I asked. "What happened? Where am I?"

Everything was a blur. There were faces out there and something over my mouth. For a second I thought I was dead. Then I saw shapes moving, and somebody was shouting. That wasn't my idea of being dead, so I tried to sit up.

"Nick's waking up," I heard somebody say.

Then there was a big rush. All the shapes and faces began to move. I tried to focus, but it was hard.

"Hey, Nick, it's me," I heard. I remembered that voice. And then the face came into focus.

"Marco!" I said. "You're not dead."

"Hey, man. Neither are you." Then Marco started to laugh.

Other faces gathered around. There was my mom and my little brother. My mom looked like she'd been crying. My brother was just jumping up and down.

"What . . . what happened?" I asked.

"The firemen got us all out – you, me, Rosa."

"Rosa?"

"Yeah, remember we were supposed to go to that movie," Marco explained. "They came to find us and saw the house on fire. So Lee phoned 911 and Rosa tried to get us out of the kitchen, except the smoke got to her first. But the firemen got there just in time, and they brought us all out."

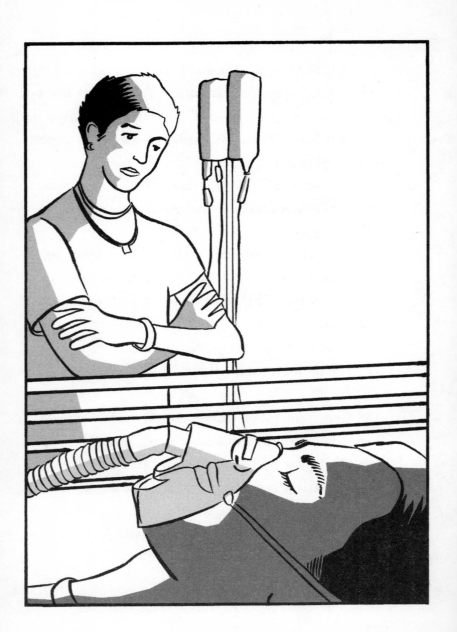

"So is Rosa, like, okay?" I asked.

"Yeah, she went home already. You, Nick, you've been out of it for two days."

That's when Jackson spoke up. "We thought you were gonna die!"

"Oh, Jackson," my mom cut in, "the doctors said he'd come around. And here you are, as good as new."

Actually, I didn't feel as good as new. I had this mask to help me breathe, and my head was all fuzzy. I felt weak, like I was still tied up. And then I remembered all that – the Russian guys, being tied up and the fire.

"What about the Russian guys?" I asked. "Did they catch 'em?"

"Yeah, Lee got the license plate number. The cops picked them up pretty fast. And guess what? They're not Russian, they're Polish."

So much for my skill in language.

"Were they working for Re-Nu?"

"Looks like it. Of course that guy we met,

Liddell, he says he never saw them before. I guess it will all come out in court."

"Yeah, I guess," I sighed.

"I've got a little more news for you, buddy," Marco went on. "I think Rosa is getting some kind of medal for trying to save us."

"She's a hero!" Jackson added.

Marco shook his head. "Yeah, it was kind of stupid to rush into a burning building, but at least she tried." He waited for a second, then spoke again. "And you know what else?"

"What?"

"Rosa kind of likes you," he said, grinning at me. "She says we should try the movie thing again . . . when you get back on your feet. She thinks you're cute, Nick – at least with an air mask on your face."

Check out these other EDGE novels

 **Behind the Door** by Paul Kropp. Jamal and his buddies like to hang out in the basement of an old warehouse. Things are cool until a strange door appears on an inside wall. Of course, the guys have to look behind the door — and then the horror begins.

 **Outrage** by Tony Varrato. Connor's had a rough day — punched out by a buddy, kicked out of school, beaten up on the way home. And then he gets accused of robbing a corner store. It all sucks, big time.

 **Turf War** by Alex Kropp. Kasim and his friends aren't much of a gang. They're not like Crips or Bloods, they're just a bunch of guys who hang togther. But that doesn't stop the Parkside Prep guys when they decide to clean up the Edge.

Paul Kropp is the author of many popular novels for young people. His work includes nine novels for young adults, many high-interest novels, and other work for adults and younger children.

Mr. Kropp's best-known novel for young adults, *Moonkid and Liberty* and *Moonkid and Prometheus*, have been translated into many languages and won awards around the world. His two most recent novels are *Running the Bases* and *Homerun*, both published by Doubleday Canada. For more information, see the author's website at www.paulkropp.com.

NO TEACHERS ALLOWED:
For online discussion of HIP Edge novels and characters, student readers are invited to the HIP Edge Café.
www.hip-edge-cafe.com

For more information on HIP novels:

High Interest Publishing – Publishers of EDGE novels
407 Wellesley Street East • Toronto, Ontario M4X 1H5
www.hip-books.com